Dear Jeremy,

May you have countless hours of pleasure reading this book to your darling daughter.

Love,
Sue - Alan

# DADDY'S SONG

**Lesléa Newman** ✦ illustrated by **Karen Ritz**

Henry Holt and Company ✦ New York

*For Dad, with love on your 80th birthday*—L. N.

*To the spirit and encouragement of my dear friend,*
*Barbara Knutson*—K. R.

Henry Holt and Company, LLC
*Publishers since 1866*
175 Fifth Avenue
New York, New York 10010
www.henryholtchildrensbooks.com

Library of Congress Cataloging-in-Publication Data
Newman, Lesléa.
Daddy's song / Lesléa Newman; illustrated by Karen Ritz.—1st ed.
p.    cm.
Summary: At bedtime, a father conjures up images of all sorts of strange things that could happen—
from ice cream cones falling from the sky to penguins jumping on trampolines—
but no matter what, he and his love will be there.
ISBN-13: 978-0-8050-6975-4 / ISBN-10: 0-8050-6975-5
[1. Father and child—Fiction. 2. Love—Fiction. 3. Bedtime—Fiction. 4. Stories in rhyme.] I. Ritz, Karen, ill. II. Title.
PZ8.3.N4655Dad 2007    [E]—dc22    2006007607

First Edition—2007 / Designed by Patrick Collins
The artist used gouache on 40 lb. Fabriano paper to create the illustrations for this book.
Printed in the United States of America on acid-free paper. ∞

1   3   5   7   9   10   8   6   4   2

Before I tuck you in tonight,
Kiss your cheek and shut the light,
The last thing left for me to do
Is sing my Daddy's song to you.

If ice cream cones fall from the sky,

And cats grow wings and start to fly,

If foxes play with balls and bats,
And chickens wear fine coats and hats,

If reindeer ride in fancy cars,
And rabbits leap among the stars,

If pigs and bears play hide-and-seek,

And cows and horses learn to speak...

If snow falls down in purple flakes,
And kangaroos bake birthday cakes,

If crickets build a house of bricks,
And monkeys practice magic tricks,

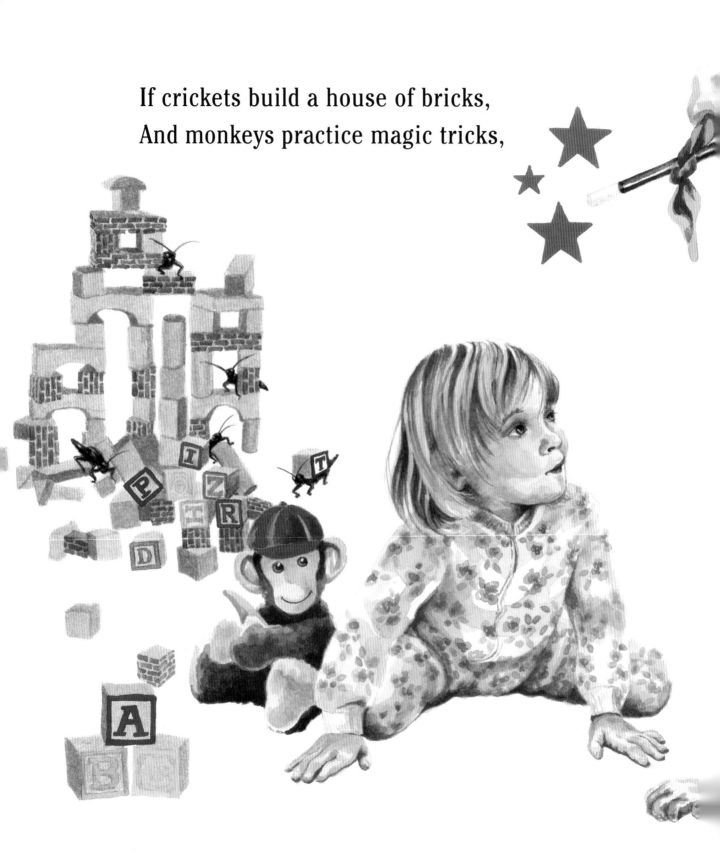

If panda bears twirl hula hoops,
And ducks and lions sail in sloops,

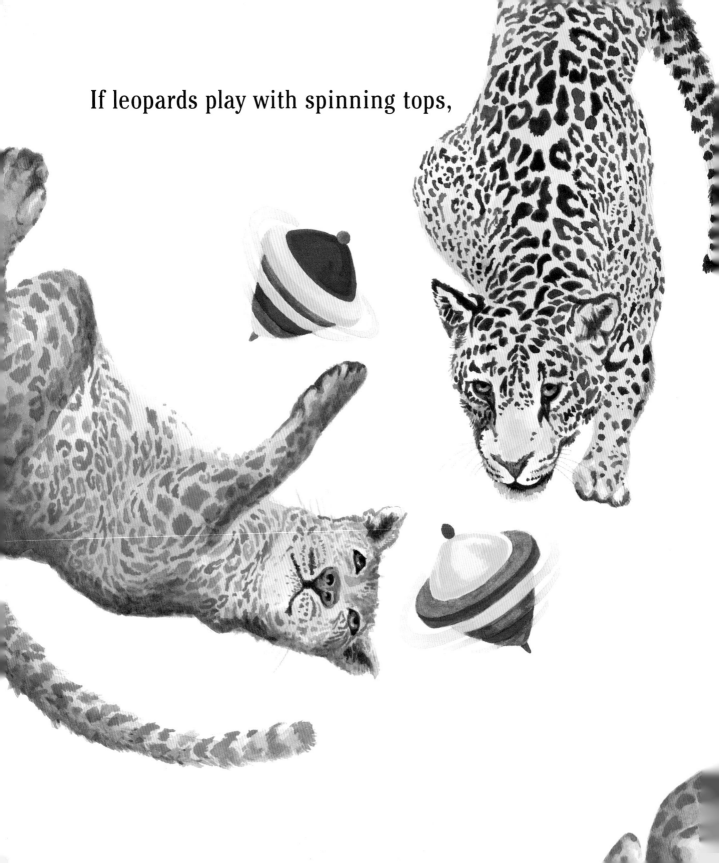

If leopards play with spinning tops,

And frogs and turtles run the shops . . .

If rain falls up instead of down,
And turkeys ride their bikes to town,

If dogs play checkers in the park,
And sheep go camping in the dark,

If elephants ride carousels,
And tigers play trombones and bells,

If walruses eat jelly beans,
And penguins jump on trampolines . . .

If this whole world turns inside out
And silly things are all about,
Remember what will still be true—

Your daddy's here,
and he loves you.